Adelaide's Secret World

Elise Hurst

Alfred A. Knopf
New York

To Erica and Elise, with infinite love

Adelaide lived in a little old shop
behind a soft red curtain.

Once it had been a bustling place, full of wonders.

But over time, Adelaide
found herself all alone,
and the quiet stillness
crept into her heart
and stayed.

Every morning, Adelaide watched the sun rise and the ships come into port.

Every night, she listened to the hum of the setting
sun and the soft pure song of the evening star.

By day, she would look out for the still ones,
the quiet ones, those who danced
and sighed and dreamed alone.

And at home, her head full of their stories,
Adelaide would work into the night, taking
a little bit of the world and making it her own.

But there was always something missing.

One day, Adelaide was restless. She set off
under a brooding sky. Buildings rose around
her and disappeared into the gray.
Everyone scurried and rushed.

Suddenly the sky growled.

Adelaide saw Fox dart away,
his special book knocked
to the ground.

Adelaide didn't stop to think.
She scooped up the book and followed Fox,
through twists and turns, to a little green door.

The rain-soaked windows glittered like a jewelry box.
Peering in, Adelaide could see Fox's world,
drawings scattered around the room.
And she knew them all—the dancers, the lost ones,
the midnight cat, and herself, Adelaide.

The door opened, but though
her heart called out, she
could make no sound.

Adelaide ran.

She burst through her door,
tearing the curtain.
As it unraveled, the wind rushed in.

Adelaide's world tumbled and spun.

As the storm
died down,
Adelaide knew
what to do.

When the day dawned, the city had changed.
There was music and laughter.
Ones became twos.
Twos became fours.

And those who had once
been lonely and silent . . .

. . . found their
voices.

THIS IS A BORZOI BOOK PUBLISHED BY ALFRED A. KNOPF

Copyright © 2015 by Elise Hurst

Visit us on the Web! randomhousekids.com

Educators and librarians, for a variety of teaching tools,
visit us at RHTeachersLibrarians.com

Library of Congress Cataloging-in-Publication Data is available upon request.
ISBN 978-1-5247-1454-3 (trade) — ISBN 978-1-5247-1455-0 (lib. bdg.) — ISBN 978-1-5247-1456-7 (ebook)

MANUFACTURED IN CHINA

February 2018
10 9 8 7 6 5 4 3 2 1
First American Edition